RODDY GOES TO CHURCH

Church Life and Church People

Canon Osborne is widely known and loved for his lifelong, faithful and effective ministry. His latest work is a unique spoof on church life. Will you recognise yourself and your church here? Your Vicar will love this. It should be compulory reading for all aspiring clergy. Derek Osborne's mind here is insightful, his characters graphic and typical and the style acutely comical, but there is a serious message in his madness. Buy this, read it and enjoy!"

Bishop David Pytches, Chorleywood

RODDY GOES TO CHURCH
Church Life and Church People

by

Derek Osborne

PUBLISHED BY
WHITE TREE PUBLISHING
28 FALLODON WAY
BRISTOL BS9 4HX
UNITED KINGDOM

For
Hilary
Jeremy, Mark, Sarah
and their families

And thanks to Caroline Clipsom, top secretary,
and to White Tree Publishing for encouragement,
advice and expertise

ABOUT THE AUTHOR

Derek Osborne is a retired Church of England minister and an Honorary Canon of Norwich Cathedral. He is married to Hilary, and together they have worked in a variety of parishes. They also served on the Chaplaincy Team of Lee Abbey, the Christian Community in North Devon which welcomes thousands of guests each year, and have made annual return visits there to lead Bible teaching weeks. Derek and Hilary have three children and seven grandchildren, and live in Cromer — where there is, praise God, a vibrant church life!

Copies of this book can be purchased from websites of major internet booksellers, or from:

Norwich Christian Resource Centre   (P&P extra)
St Michael at Plea
Redwell Street
Norwich
NR2 4SN
Tel: 01603 619731
norwichcrc@btconnect.com
www.norwichcrc.co.uk

Introduction

A few years ago, *The Times* invited a number of contributors to make a personal choice of books published in their lifetime which, for them, "showed the way". Among them, Bel Mooney, Malcolm Bradbury, Roger Scruton, A.S. Byatt, Antonia Fraser chose, respectively, works by Sylvia Plath, Saul Bellow, T.S. Eliot, Iris Murdoch and Hugh Trevor-Roper — along with other writers whom they had also found profoundly influential.

Their succinct appreciations made fascinating reading. But none more so than the offering occupying pride of place on the lead-page, headed "Felipe Fernández-Armesto says thanks to Noddy". Preceding the writer's commendations of Iris Murdoch's novel, *The Nice and the Good* and Joseph Needham's *Science and Civilisation in China* came the following, introductory, paragraphs:

> Influences which last longest start in childhood. Thanks to Enid Blyton's *Noddy* books, I still overvalue personal independence, love the underdog, crave cakes at teatime and mistrust Mr Plod.
>
> The writer has been reviled for undemanding language: but you don't notice that when you're patronised by everybody and baby-talk seems the natural form of adult expression.
>
> She has been condemned as politically incorrect, but Toy Town is nothing if not a plural society, where Sally Skittle and the Wobbly Man are unencumbered

by their disabilities. Her books are not well written, but their greatness lies in the depiction of character. Noddy is one of the most under-esteemed creations in English literature: a subtle, complex personality, whose moodiness, selective arrogance and wildness of judgment repeatedly test the affection of his readers and friends.

Busybodies may banish him from the shelves, but his place in tradition is secure.

Felipe Fernández-Armesto's piece is surmounted by a full-colour reproduction cover of the story which, he writes, "I love best … *Noddy and the Bumpy Dog* (1957) — a typical fable in which the under-appreciated outsider, 'waggy and licky and noisy and rough' — saves the day and wins acceptance."

The writer of this book acknowledges the writing of Enid Blyton, and the copyright and registered trademarks that belong to Enid Blyton Ltd, and shares the above opinion of the contribution of Noddy® from Toy Town to English literature. But in these pages we find the imaginary town of Playville, the home of Roddy who lives in a similarly plural society where *his* various friends are unencumbered by their disabilities — but not unaffected by problems related to political correctness and, of all things, religion and church life…

Chapter 1

Roddy Has a Horrid Day

Roddy was a complex but on the whole, happy little fellow. He was called Roddy because his wooden head, with a woolly pointy red hat with its small metal ball on the end, was supported by a neat wooden rod which formed his neck. When he was smiley and enjoying life, which was most of the time, he swivelled his head cheerfully, looking this way and that. But today, late afternoon, he was in a bad mood. So, looking straight ahead fixedly, he went to see his friend Bushy-Beard for comfort and tea and cakes.

Bushy-Beard was much older than Roddy and very wise. He had rosy cheeks and kind, crinkly eyes but not much hair on *top* of his head.

"'Hell is other people'. Nietzsche was dead right," proclaimed Roddy arrogantly as he sank into an armchair. "He obviously lived here, in this benighted town, all his life."

Bushy-Beard, who had been elected Mayor of Playville several times, demurred. "Steady on, Roddy. It's a good place to live. Plural society. Everyone accepts everyone else for who they are... By the way, Sartre not Nietzsche."

"Rubbish!" retorted Roddy irritably. "And I don't care if it was Plato, or Churchill, or the Pope or Ella Fitzgerald. Get real, B-B. Like it or not, you and I are trapped in a *dysfunctional* society. *Plural*, my eye!"

Bushy-Beard could tell that his little friend was not his usual happy self. "Roddy, I wonder why you are not your usual happy self today?" he queried, and added, curious,

"And why Ella Fitzgerald…?"

"My day, my whole day," snapped Roddy in reply, "has been wrecked by idiots: stupid people doing stupid things, from the crack of dawn onwards. I can't bear to remember that only last night, merely eighteen hours ago, I fell into deep sleep, soothed by the voice of Ella on CD. *She'd* understand—"

"Ah! And now, this afternoon, you are overcome by Not-OK feelings. Would you like to talk about it? My time is yours. I'm here to listen. That's what friends are for…" Bushy-Beard was slipping into his Person-Centred-Counselling mode.

"Oh spare me the empathic, unconditional, positive-regard stuff. I'm past that. Way past it."

"So what *did* happen at dawn?" persisted Bushy-Beard, unperturbed.

"In the small hours in fact. I was jerked out of dreamless, healing slumber by that milkman-from-hell, Mr Bottle, who thought it was morning. Bushy-Beard, it is a terrible, terrible experience to hear his take on Pavarotti at any time. But the excruciating cruelty of *Nessun Dorma* accompanied by crashing glass, at dead of night, when you're actually *lost* in sleep already, is a savage irony that Verdi could never have intended."

"He was only doing his job — in his usual cheery way," murmured Bushy-Beard. "Puccini."

In full flow, Roddy ignored the correction. "The man is a pain. And so is Mr Spanner. It's after breakfast. My car won't start. Clearly, it's going to be one of those days. I phone his garage. He comes round, peers under the bonnet, tut-tutting for hours on end, then, 'The big end has gone', he crows momentously — like he's solved the Irish problem. That's all I need."

"I'm sorry. That is serious," guessed Bushy-Beard.

"Stop pretending," cried Roddy, rudely. "You don't know

the first thing about big ends. Nor about rabid dogs or demented children."

"Come again?"

"There I am, car-less, relaxing in my garden in the morning sunlight, drawing comfort from the tranquillity — and with terrifying suddenness, out of nowhere, this enormous black dog leaps over my hedge barking like an artillery barrage, feet thudding like horse's hooves. Cerberus *redivivus*. The hound is pursued by a horde of shrieking children — bursting *through* the hedge, please note — and chased by their large mothers, Tilly Tenpin and Bessie Bear, braying with hysterical laughter.

"The creature tears round and round like a canine tornado, devastating everything in its path. My hollyhocks and hydrangeas, like Binsey Poplars, '*all felled, felled, are all felled*'. Stampeding kids trample anything left standing, exciting the crazed animal further with ever louder shouts of 'Bonzo, Bonzo!'"

Roddy paused.

"At that precise moment," he resumed, dramatically, "the gate of the front garden is pushed open by, of all people, Mademoiselle Fifi — all pink and frilly and hatty and high heels, as usual. It turns out she'd come to see me about a lift to the station in my car next week.

Confronted by this scene of total destruction she is rooted to the spot, and turns deathly pale. '*Zut alors!*' she cries — then, catching sight of the huge, black, bounding beast, she screams in terror — '*Eeeeek! Quelle horreur! Un chien enragé*'."

"'You can say that again,' I mutter, when the animal leaps straight towards her — seeing the open gate behind her, I suppose.

"She turns tail and totters desperately towards the gap, at speed. But — you're not going to believe this, Bushy-Beard — she collides with Percy Postman who chooses that very moment to bring me a letter. They both fall to the ground in a heap. The dog jumps over them, then somersaults back playfully and joins in the game, licking their faces with slobbering affection. Mademoiselle Fifi faints. Percy Postman probably wishes *he* could faint — you may or may not know, Bushy-Beard, that he is terrified of *all* dogs. As it is, he starts to yell with fear, no words — just yells; then crumples, soundlessly, a broken man. Nightmare. But this is how my day began… Apocalypse Now."

After a moment or two, Bushy-Beard broke the heavy silence. "Am I hearing, behind your account, hurt feelings … bitterness … anger, even…?"

"Damn right you are."

"Very understandable, my friend… What do you think, as of now, with hindsight that is, might have been an appropriate response?" asked Bushy-Beard, non-directively.

"Slaughter," replied Roddy. "Shoot the dog. Lock up the children. In fact, I did nothing. Couldn't move. Watched Percy crawl away. Mademoiselle Fifi came to, got up, straightened her clothes, patted her hair and clip-clopped off, white as a sheet, clutching her hat. The dog and kids and mothers had disappeared.

"The whole episode had been surreal. I remained where I was in the deckchair, paralysed with Meaninglessness — like someone out of Kafka. Stared straight in front of me, motionless, for hours. At noon, I rallied, stumbled into the kitchen, munched through four bags of crisps, three doughnuts and a bar of chocolate, swallowed a litre of Coca Cola and went to bed. You will understand, Bushy-Beard, why you see before you someone in the grip of Post Traumatic Stress Disorder."

It crossed his friend's mind that the disorder was equally related to indigestion, but realising that this would have been due to comfort-eating, said nothing. Instead, intuiting that Roddy's narrative was unfinished —

"Is that it?" he asked gently. "No. I sense there is more…"

"Worse. You ain't heard nuthin' yet," responded Roddy, though with a slightly brighter note in his voice. "This afternoon I pull myself together and decide to turn my back on chaos, take my mind off things and seek Normality by supporting the Church Fete. So off I toddle to the sports field. Terrible mistake. *Ghastly* experience. Come back, Marx, all is forgiven.

"It was one huge, depressing, capitalistic *fest*. Consumerism gone mad. Rampant materialism. Stall holders everywhere, rooking the public, raking in lolly by the cartload. Most demeaning of all, *bric-a-brac* — ancient jigsaw puzzles, discarded baby-clothes, defunct record-players, picture frames with no glass, dead clocks, chipped cups and saucers, frightful old watercolours — you name it. And simple souls stumping up like it was the Antiques Road Show.

"Then, every few yards, someone waving raffle tickets in your face. Who in their right senses would *want* to win first prize of a day-trip to Toyville? Masochism!"

Roddy paused, but only for a moment. "But it wasn't just the dead hand of greed. Anarchy ruled."

Bushy-Beard raised his eyebrows. "You really *are* in a bad way. First, some harmless retail therapy gets maligned. Now, wild accusations of anarchy — *anarchy?* — at Playville's annual family festival day…?"

"On every side, Bushy-Beard. Take the races and their aftermath. Mr Top-Heavy and the huge Ernie Elephant tried to organise races for the children, but kept bumping into each other and falling over. None of the kids ever got to running; just rampaged around the place fighting and shrieking. That made some of their dads hopping mad and it led to a shouting match among them, about who should take over — though I could see it was that villainous pair of gremlins, Shifty and Sarky, who were stirring up the trouble and encouraging rivalry.

"PC Boots rocked up and down on his heels, glaring, looking like he wanted to arrest everybody in sight. Meantime, Miss Prickly-Cat prowled around the stalls, angrily lashing her tail and muttering, in her top-drawer voice, something incomprehensible about 'worldly methods' and some guy called 'Mammon' — and occasionally she even swiped out with her handbag, like the original Iron Lady.

"Then, about mid-afternoon, when I joined loads of others entering the marquee for tea, Porky Pig and Dennis Donkey between them pulled up all the guy-rope pegs and the whole thing collapsed on top of us. You never heard such a cacophony. It took me twenty minutes to extricate myself, and run.

"I have since learned that everyone survived. But the whole event was less than a successful, harmonious occasion, Bushy-Beard. The End of the World will be a picnic by comparison to this afternoon. And you're telling me that this is 'a good place to live'. Sheer hubris, my friend. Dante got it right: 'All hope abandon, ye who enter here'."

Bushy-Beard regarded Roddy sternly. "Things are not as bad as they seem to you," he said. "I was there myself this afternoon and it was all very jolly. Great success. It was a pity about the marquee. Silly practical joke — not funny. But that was minor. In general, the whole afternoon went very well. You have looked upon it with a jaundiced eye. Your windows of perception were muddied by the unfortunate experiences of the morning. You *entered* the fete with a negative life-script. The Child in you was swamping the Adult, and your arrogant Parent is making matters worse by—!"

Bushy-Beard was warming to his theme but Roddy shut him up. "Bushy-Beard, you are talking a load of nonsense."

"And you, Roddy," rejoined Bushy-Beard firmly, "are not

yourself. You are out of sorts."

Roddy fell silent. He knew his friend was right. "Well, how do you get back *into* sorts?" he asked, miserably. "Anyway," he added, reflectively "What *are* 'sorts'?"

Bushy-Beard stroked his beard thoughtfully. "Perhaps," he replied, hesitantly, "perhaps you need a fresh start, new interests. A different dimension to life. Perhaps you should come to church."

"*WHAT*?!" gasped Roddy.

Chapter 2

Roddy Goes to Church

It was all rather odd, because church doesn't usually feature in narratives about life in Playville — or in similar towns, come to that. "Religion doesn't sit comfortably with the customary storyline," Roddy reminded Bushy-Beard.

"Well, that's just it!" Bushy-Beard replied excitedly. "*That's* the trouble. The medium is the message. We *all* lose the plot. Hence existential angst. 'Confusion worse confounded' as Shakespeare said—"

"Milton. Paradise Lost," retaliated Roddy. "But I don't see what church has got to do with it."

"Church, Roddy, represents *sanity* — truth and order. Relationships rooted in Reality: which is what we need. That's what we're here for — 'Only Connect'…"

"You mean Paradise Regained equals Come-and-Join-Us-On-Sundays where everything is hunky-dory?"

Bushy-Beard looked uneasy. "Well, hardly that. No, hardly that. But I think you need what's on offer, Roddy — or, rather, to meet the Person at the heart of it all. How about it: next Sunday — tomorrow in fact — eleven o'clock?"

Roddy had stared unbelievingly at his be-whiskered friend. "OK," he promised finally. "I'll give it a whirl."

"Well, aren't you glad you went along?" asked Bushy-Beard on Monday morning. "You look more like yourself today."

He and Roddy were enjoying coffee and doughnuts in

Bushy-Beard's cosy, shabby lounge. Roddy was indeed back to a more equable frame of mind. He welcomed the invitation to share reflections on his visit to Playville Parish Church the day before.

"Yes, B-B," he agreed, with cheerful seriousness and, choosing his words carefully, "It was all very ... interesting. In fact, *mesmerising* is the word that comes to mind. Yep, I do feel better for going. And I was agreeably surprised. For one thing, I hadn't realised so many townsfolk would be there. But I have lots of questions..."

"Fire away."

Roddy reached for another doughnut. "Why," he queried, licking sugar from his fingers, "why do you have all those books? It wasn't easy. Miss Prickly-Cat was inside the door — she seemed a bit surprised to see me — perhaps 'shaken' is the word — and snarled at me, though, to be fair, she may have been smiling. You can't really tell. She ordered me to take my hat off, so I did, and dropped it, and the bobble rattled on the floor, and she said, 'Ssshh'. I picked it up and put it under one arm and said 'Sorry', and she said 'Ssshh' again, and then thrust about twenty-five books under the other arm."

"A hyperbole," smiled Bushy-Beard. "But let it pass. Let it pass."

"Well, hyperbole or not, I stagger down your — *aisle*, I think you call it — feeling like a cross between a hat-rack and a mobile library. I just about make it to an empty bench — sorry, pew — quite near the front and then drop the whole pile with an almighty crash. To my consternation, Mr Top-Heavy who's sitting on the pew in front of me, leaning forward in a kind of devout crouch, face in his hands, leaps to his feet with a startled cry at the sudden noise and topples over into the pew in front of *him*... Just then, the Vicar-man comes in, in black and white like a penguin, and says we all have to sing a hymn."

Roddy paused for breath.

"By the time I've found the right book, two things have happened — (a) everybody has stopped singing and (b) to my dismay, Miss Prickly-Cat comes and stands next to me.

"'Roddy,' she hisses, 'you should not be here'. I wasn't sure what she meant. Being in a nervous state of heightened spiritual tension, I thought at first she meant that my existence was some kind of dreadful cosmic mistake. Then I concluded that I ought not to be there, in the church. But then she growled under her breath, 'This is *my* pew — the Cat Family Pew'.

"Evidently, I learned afterwards, generations of Prickly-Cat types have sat there for hundreds of years — since the beginning. The rest of the building was probably put up around them. You can imagine the workmen covering them with dust sheets when they were plastering the walls. Anyway, there was nothing I could do except mutter 'Sorry' again — very quietly — and resume searching through my assorted volumes, with her giving me exasperated side-long glances.

"Then I thought everything would be OK because, as you know, the Vicar-man stopped reading stuff out loud and turned to us and smiled, stretched out his white, sheeted arms — looking like a holy ghost — and said something about Peace, and everyone started shaking hands with each other. So I smiled nervously at Miss Prickly-Cat and held out my hand. She looked pretty cross and snapped, 'Don't be ridiculous. We're *supposed* to be here for higher things,' and she knelt down abruptly as though she'd been knee-capped. I didn't know how to react. But then it *was* OK, because a whole lot of others crowded round and were ever so friendly and huggy and said jolly things like 'God bless you, Roddy' and 'Great to see you here. Welcome!' — including you, Bushy-Beard and the Vicar-man."

"Well, there you are then," said Bushy-Beard. "As I said,

there's a lot of genuine friendliness in our church."

"Well, yes… Except it didn't seem to me exactly *child*-friendly," responded Roddy thoughtfully. "Cool it is not. I actually felt sorry — would you believe it — for the Tenpin kids and Mrs Bear's lot, and the others. I wondered how *they* coped with all those books. And the hymns were nothing like the songs they sing in school — no noticeably funky beat — and the tunes were so high and screechy. You could see that they were trying, bless them — everyone was trying. It was painful. And when we got to those weird chanted-numbers, it sounded like the drones and shrieks of a Tibetan funeral dirge…

"And, continuing on a musical note — so to speak — the *organ*! You've *got to do something about it*. It is in terminal decline. And not even PC Boots will keep it alive — with all his frantic attempts at resuscitation. I could see him at the rear of it pumping like mad, but several times it descended from asthmatic squeaky noises to terrible dying wails. Constable Boots is not as young as he was, and there he was, red-faced, apoplectic — puffing fit to bust. There'll be dying wails from *him* after a few more Sundays. For heaven's sake, can't you install an electric blowing machine or something?"

Bushy-Beard looked uncomfortable. "That's very difficult, Roddy," he replied. "It's a bone of contention within the church family. A Cause of Division. You have unknowingly stumbled upon an Issue which is provoking Great Pain. Indeed, it has even led to angry words being exchanged, and irate letters to the Vicar. The whole situation is very fraught — unworthily so."

Roddy was mystified. His genial friend had dropped into that embarrassingly pompous way of speaking which sometimes took him over. "B-B, you've got a bad attack of gravitas again. What on earth are you rabbiting on about? And what's all this about writing letters? Why on earth don't people call and talk to the man?"

"Good point. But, you see, it's like this, Roddy," continued Bushy-Beard resignedly. "The matter of the organ has come before the Church Council more than once. Some of us want to do as you suggest — electrify the instrument, so to speak. Others, though, object — strongly: they feel it would be irreverent——"

Roddy, who was drinking his coffee, spluttered and hastily put his mug down. "*Irreverent?*" he gasped incredulously. "*Irreverent?* You mean they reckon God would be mad?"

"Well, sort of, I suppose. Though they wouldn't put it that way," replied Bushy-Beard.

"But why? The angels must be driven crazy by that terrible racket invading heaven every Sunday morning. I can imagine Gabriel shuddering and covering his ears. The harpists must be feeling wrung out. And no one up there can be too happy about PC Boots shortening his life-span — he nearly slipped this mortal coil yesterday. That last hymn went on forever."

"Alas," responded Bushy-Beard, "Constable Boots is a leading member of the Party Opposing, and he is also the Church Council's vice-chairman. And Miss Prickly-Cat is the secretary. Need I say more? You will not be surprised that they hold strong views. They declare, forcibly, that it would be wrong, theologically and spiritually, to equip the organ with artificial, scientific power — such worldly methods would fly in the face of all that the church stands for, and go against centuries of tradition for no good reason. The pair of them have even threatened to write to the Bishop."

"You cannot be serious!" Roddy captured perfectly the McEnroe tone of pained incredulity. Then: "But the *light bulbs* — you've got electric lights! For heaven's sake, do you all beseech divine forgiveness every time you switch them on? Why hasn't the whole system been fused by a thunderbolt by now?"

Bushy-Beard looked even more uncomfortable. "Perhaps I should not say this, Roddy, but yes, there is, I agree, an element of illogical rationalisation about the Opposition's case which, I fear, disguises a more fundamental, *subjective* reason for their implacable stance."

"You mean," guessed Roddy, "it's because PC Boots would be out of a job? He'd lose his status-fulfilment and all that? That's what you're all scared about — making a martyr of him — like Ridley and Cranmer?"

Bushy-Beard was rather thrown by Roddy's parallel, feeling that it was overstated and lacked appositeness. But remembering that his friend's knowledge of the English Reformation was minimal, he replied, "Well, you could say that. But there's more to it — as you found with Miss Prickly-Cat, the matter goes back into history. The Constable's father, grandfather and great-grandfather before him all pumped the organ in their time..."

"Exactly!" cried Roddy. "It's a power thing — in more senses than one. Closed shop. Security of tenure. 'Who runs this church — you or me? Me! — my family — always has done. Along with the Prickly-Cats'"

"You're on the right track," admitted Bushy-Beard. "As you can surmise, she — with him — is also vehemently against getting rid of the pews. But that's another matter."

"Golly!" exclaimed Roddy, "I can see that *would* upset the apple-cart. But listen — about the organ — why doesn't the Vicar-man tell them where to get off? He's the boss. He should set Bonzo onto them." (Roddy had discovered, with mixed feelings, that Bonzo was, in fact, the Vicarage dog)

"Oh Roddy, how can he do that? This is such a close-knit community, as you well know. It's not just those two who object: there are others. Anyway, it would not be a loving thing to do"

"Rhubarb!" retorted Roddy, impatiently, but added, "I do begin to feel sorry for the Vicar-man, though. He seems a really decent guy. I liked what he said from the pulpit — made a lot of sense: practical, down to earth, but a lot of God in it too. Yes, I'll admit it really got to me."

Roddy paused.

"Bushy-Beard," he continued eventually, "it *was* a lousy day for me last Saturday — you've got to agree. But OK, I was a bit over-grumpy. More than once recently I haven't felt too proud of myself. It's encouraging to be reminded that we can change … like he said yesterday"

"You're getting the message, Roddy," commented Bushy-Beard gently. "And," he added, "there are quite a few changes for the better that the Vicar would like to see in the church — changes you'd approve of, Roddy, because he's got the children in mind, especially — and the music! But it's not easy for him — not easy at all. You're new to the church, Roddy, and so is he — only arrived a few months ago — so why not get to know him and encourage him?"

Roddy drained his coffee and rose to his feet. "OK, B-B, I think I will. Thanks for the doughnuts. Be seeing you."

"One more thing," said Bushy-Beard, as his friend turned to the door, "there's a Public Meeting about the organ and related matters on Wednesday next week. It's called a Hearing. Boffins from the diocese are coming. Might be a bit heavy. But it's open to everyone. You could come, if you'd like to."

Roddy left Bushy-Beard's house and walked home thoughtfully along Playville High Street.

Chapter 3

Roddy Attends the Hearing

The church, for that is where the Public Meeting was held, was crowded. On the front of the chancel stood a long table behind which were seated a number of diocesan dignitaries. Centrally placed, as Chairman, was the Archdeacon. After his rather unctuous welcome to everyone present, and less than succinct statement of what was being proposed in relation to the organ, and the purpose of the Hearing, he declared the matter open to contributions from the floor.

The first speaker, rising to his feet with some alacrity, was Shifty, the senior of the two gremlins. "Your Venerableness, Mr Mayor, fellow-citizens of Playville, may I, on behalf of the Party Opposing, come straight to the point. Behind this debate concerning music in our church lies an ecclesiological — indeed, theological — issue of vital and far-reaching significance, for it impinges not only upon this parish but, by extension, upon the distinctive identity and global mission of that great worldwide Communion of which we are proud to be a part and of which you, Mr Archdeacon, are an honoured figurehead and guardian among us. The key question to be addressed this evening is this — *What kind of church should we be, in this day and age?* What constitutes our authenticity? How shall we be perceived by our un-churched neighbours? What about our professed concern for peoples in other lands, of every tribe and nation — indeed, those already among us who do not share our heritage? Above all, is not our *theology* in serious danger of being compromised, and," he added darkly, "our *leadership* led astray? Will we be inveigled into liberalism and blunder into the quicksands of postmodern relativism? Or are we to stand where we have always stood, unswayed by emotionally-determined argument, true to our time-honoured traditions, unyielding in our allegiance to the means and methods established by our forebears...?"

He said a lot more along the same lines and sat down.

"What's all that got to do with the organ?" whispered Roddy to Bushy-Beard.

As if he had heard Roddy's question, the other gremlin, Sarky, stood up. "Mr Chairman, I stand to support our good friend Shifty and to thank him for his profoundly perceptive and moving speech. He has rightly shown us the importance of the Big Picture — the all-important extensive ramifications of this evening's decisions. I now wish, in my remarks, to dwell upon the *specific* focal point of these considerations — the organ itself. *But*, in particular, upon the poignant *human* factors involved. Supremely, these have their sharpest focus in our dear brother Police Constable Boots. I trust we all realise that he has been deeply wounded by this painful controversy. May we assure him, Mr Archdeacon, of our heartfelt sympathy and unqualified esteem. The deplorable, hurtful criticism implicit in the attitude of those who would dispense with his services must indeed have been hard to bear. Without his persevering, indefatigable pumping week by week, the sound of music from our organ would have ceased long ago — *sic transit gloria mundi.* And what would have followed — what *could* follow — such an unthinkable eventuality? Remember Shifty's eloquent warnings about the grim consequences of loosening our moorings. What next? Electric guitars? Honky-tonk in the chancel? Pop groups howling across these hallowed pews? Anthems replaced by banal ditties and hypnotic mantras? Dancing in the aisles? Are not unspeakable developments like these but the logical extension of an *electrically-powered organ*? Indeed, shall we shortly see this much-loved ancient instrument displaced by a *completely* electronic device called, I believe, a *synthesiser*?"

"O, I say, steady on!"

The man next to the Archdeacon, who was the Diocesan Chief Clerk jumped to his feet behind the table, straightened his legal wig and declared, "Let us be quite clear. In relation to the present organ we are not here to discuss *replacement*, which is out of the question. Its demise cannot be contemplated. Rather, we are here to consider the pros and cons of prophylactic enhancement by mechanical means. In the event of application being made for such an operation, it is very possible that the diocese *would* issue appropriate authorisation. But imagine what would ensue if our Faculties were replaced by Death Certificates in such cases as this."

Roddy was startled. But before Bushy-Beard could explain the difference between ecclesiastical and medical vocabularies, old Colonel Gunshot stood up, erect, moustaches bristling.

"*Dammit!*" he began, uncompromisingly. "Can't see what all the fuss is about. Know your enemy! Establish Objectives! Identify Obstacles! Eliminate them! Praise the Lord! Read the Good Book! Pray like mad! Sing your heart out — cheers up the chaps, organ or no organ. Important thing is to keep Rome out! No popery! *Dammit!*"

"I do so agree with everything that has been said," pronounced Bessie Bear bravely, holding onto the top of the pew in front of her. "What I think is that we should all love one another. Like Harry Secombe used to sing. You know…" — she struggled to recall the words, which she got wrong anyway — "'Love is a highly-coloured thing, like the April showers that bring the flowers in the early Spring'.

After all, everyone wants the best. I think we should thank our Vicar and PC Boots and Deirdre Doll our organist — and you, your Worship," she added, curtseying to the Archdeacon before she sat down.

"And how much expense would this electrical contrivance commit us to?" asked a lugubrious voice. Mr Mopey was always lugubrious. Some people said, unkindly, that his first name was Eeyore. "Thousands of pounds, I warrant. And where will you find that kind of money? Growing on trees? What about maintenance costs? In my experience, electrical gadgets are always going wrong — fuses here, worn parts there, frayed wires. More than likely it would give Miss Doll a fatal shock. Imagine the publicity — 'Church Organist Fried to Death in the Middle of a Hymn.' We'd never live it down."

"Yes, I do think there are better uses for our money," interposed Mr Moneybags, the Treasurer. "This electric motor would be an extravagant luxury which we can ill afford. And just think of those hundreds and hundreds of wretches in Toyville's cardboard city. Probably none of them has even a *harmonica* to play. We should send a donation to their Deprived Persons Mission — not waste it on modern fads."

Ernie Elephant spoke up. "That's all very well. Personally, I don't see it *is* a luxury. I'm *worried* about Constable Boots. He can't go on for ever. On his last legs, if you ask me. I don't know about Miss Doll snuffing it — the Constable's showing the strain *now*. With respect, Boots, you're not a young man anymore. What are you? Ninety-five? And I can't see anybody else likely to take over the pump. It would need to be someone much younger." He looked around, trunk waving, then fixed his eyes on Roddy, who dropped his head and slid down in the pew. Bushy-Beard glanced at him.

"It's alright, Roddy. Constable Boots can't be *that* old —

he just seems it."

To everyone's astonishment Mademoiselle Fifi, beautifully coiffeured, rose to her feet in a cloud of expensive perfume. This evening she was immaculately attired in a purple creation.

"Damned attractive woman," commented Colonel Gunshot, rather audibly, to his neighbour. "Pity she's a Frog. Easy on the eye, hard on the ear, eh what! Fine filly, though."

"*Mesdames, Messieurs*, rarely do I come to zees *église, mais j'aime la musique* which, after all is, as you say 'ere, ze food of love — *religieuse et romantique* — *mais aussi de joie. Malheureusement, vous êtes très troublés parce que notre ami Constable Boots est très fatigué, et il se peut que la mort s'approche* — it eez 'ard work Sunday after Sunday to, 'ow you say, push *l'énorme orgue. Que faire?* I 'ave *une suggestion. En France* we listen *avec grand plaisir à l'accordéon* — in English, accordion. *Cet instrument de musique* produces sounds of *joie de vivre mais aussi* solemn tears. *Aussi*, it eez portable, in ze arms. I will be 'appy to 'elp by playing my *accordion* — which I 'ave at 'ome in my 'ouse — in ze church." She sat down.

All were at a loss how to respond to Mademoiselle Fifi. The Chief Clerk sat with his head clutched between his hands. But to everyone's amazement, the Chairman rose and spoke directly to her in impeccable French. Her participation in the proceedings was greatly valued (he declared). The *entente cordiale* between our two great nations had been hugely enhanced by her heartfelt sharing of the concerns felt by the community of Playville and by her overwhelming generosity. Her offer would be seriously considered, her compassionate sympathy for the good Constable noted with gratitude. In conclusion, "*Dieu vous bénisse,*" he said.

Mademoiselle Fifi simpered.

Suddenly, a frisson of apprehension crackled through the atmosphere as Miss Prickly-Cat stood up in her place. Pursing her lips before speaking, and glaring at the Archdeacon who flinched visibly, she looked all round and addressed the company.

"My father, grandfather, great-grandfather, and great-great-grandfather have sat in the pew I now occupy tonight and every Sunday — and have been, through the years, blessed, *blessed* by the music issuing from our organ. Constable Boots' devotion — and that of *his* forefathers — in facilitating its continuing use has been a moving, challenging example to us all. And now, a dreadful act of vandalism is proposed, nay *recommended* — apparently, I cannot believe it, by our spiritual leaders — whereby this sacred instrument, with such holy associations, is to be desecrated. A modern, ugly, mechanical motor would be thrust into the heart of it and connected to the electrical mains. *Never!* Never must this be allowed to happen. Never *shall* it be allowed while I remain a member of this perfidious congregation. I do not stand alone. But I would be prepared, if necessary to stand alone, for I can do no other. Or," she concluded in an unexpectedly tearful whisper, "or — *leave*. Leave this place, leave this town…" She sank to the pew, overcome. An audible communal gasp echoed round the church.

"Good riddance!" muttered Colonel Gunshot. "Sooner the better. *Females* — hysterical, the lot of them! Except for one or two…," remembering Mademoiselle Fifi.

But most were greatly shaken by Miss Prickly-Cat's ultimatum.

"Well, if she goes, I go," harrumphed Mr Top-Heavy. Then he added, "It's a crying shame."

There were murmurs of agreement. No more contributions were forthcoming. The time had already come for the Archdeacon to sum up. He rose to his feet and looked around benignly — at the walls, pillars, windows and roof, then focused, unnervingly, on someone who wasn't there, in the back left-hand corner of the building.

"Why doesn't he look at us?" whispered Roddy.

"Don't know," replied Bushy-Beard in a low voice. "People-phobia? Perhaps he's just shy — or scared. It's a critical moment..."

Roddy thought this did not augur too well for a successful outcome to the Hearing, but said nothing.

"My heart," began the Archdeacon pompously, "my heart is warmed by the quite splendid level of debate we have all been privileged to be part of this evening. The contributions, all of an extremely high standard of cogency and — if I may say so, of articulate expression — cannot fail to have moved us forward towards a resolution of the matter before us and will lead in due time, I am confident, to a culmination marked by a common, united mind. In the meantime, yes, we do find ourselves in an exciting state of *creative tension.* I welcome this, for it is an indication of the earnestness and openness with which you are engaging in the continuing dialogue. After all, the glory of our great Communion — of which, indeed, Playville Parish Church is a vital part — is its *comprehensiveness.* We find ourselves, as we often do, holding together *two integrities.* This is a sign, if I may say so, of great maturity — that in a spirit, among you, of regard and respect, you are able to voice, with candour and sincerity, divergent views on the matter under consideration. In this way you are yourselves becoming an integral part of that *process* which will, in due time, lead, through pain, to a convergence of opinion which will be all the richer because shot through with mutual ecclesial recognition and acceptance. So this evening, once again, we are all setting out on a journey——"

"Nonsense!" barked the Colonel. "Not going anywhere. Staying here. Except for the Cat woman. That's up to her."

"… and as is always the case, we do not know our exact destination. That is not important. The important thing is our relationship with each other along the way. There is a Grand Design for us to discover or, to use a homely illustration, a *pattern* which is not at once discernible but gradually becomes evident — as when needles are employed by ladies who are er … darning." The word he was searching for was "knitting". All the women present raised scornful eyebrows at each other. The men looked at the speaker uncomprehendingly, as well they might.

"Or," continued the Archdeacon, hastily switching metaphors, "consider the musical instrument which is the subject of our common concern at this Hearing. It has contrasting keys — black and white. But the admirable Miss Doll, your organist, produces, not clashing chords, but musical harmony to entrance the ear. So it must be with us."

Unaware that his analogy was neither novel nor particularly apt in terms of its original connotation (for Playville was nothing if not a plural society), the Archdeacon developed his theme. "All that matters is the *melody* which permeates our uttered words, spoken or sung, and transcends them. As Shelley put it –

'Music, when soft voices die,
    Vibrates in the memory –
Odours, when sweet violets sicken,
    Live within the sense they quicken'
And so, among us——"

"What *is* the old fool on about now?" queried Colonel Gunshot in a loud voice to his neighbour. "Why bring in this Violet-woman — especially if the poor creature's sick. And who the blazes is Shelley when he's at home? Her husband?"

"I think he's the electrician from Toyville — the man to fix the blower," came the whispered response.

The Archdeacon was continuing his summing-up. After a few minutes Roddy, in company with many others, dropped off to sleep. He said, much later, to Bushy-Beard, that the speaker's voice sounded, through sleep, like Tennyson's 'moan of doves in immemorial elms'. Bushy-Beard agreed, but wishing to be a little more positive, quoted Wordsworth about things flashing on the inward eye *afterwards* when 'in vacant or in pensive mood...'

Bushy-Beard had in fact remained awake during the entire discourse and described the content to Roddy as a mix of stream-of-consciousness and synod-speak. In retrospect, it consisted of loosely-connected sound bites launched into the air and plopping to the floor. "Body-ministry ... truth many-sided ... mission statement ... ecclesial priorities ... visionary planning ... defining moment ... expressions of preference ... contextual relevance ... enculturation ... today's alienated young people ... the now and the not-yet ... narrative theology ... the sacred in the secular ... Phoenix-like from the ashes — LET US PRAY."

At this abrupt concluding command, issued in a sudden loud voice, Roddy had awoken with a start and, with everyone else, lurched to his feet. Afterwards, also like everyone else, he staggered home staring unseeingly ahead, completely silent. In fact, nobody said anything for days. It seemed that no one remembered the Archdeacon's address as a white-knuckle ride.

"I *think* the key phrase in his summing-up," hazarded the Vicar in the Notices the following Sunday, "was 'expressions of preference'. He advises us to have a kind of Referendum: to establish those who would approve the installation of an electric blowing motor for our organ, and those who disapprove. But before we go any further, I suggest that we need to pray. All who would like to attend are invited to a meeting for prayer at the Vicarage, every Tuesday, starting this week. Eight p.m."

Chapter 4

Roddy and the Audit

It was Roddy who suggested a Prayer Audit. They had met for three consecutive Tuesdays. They had prayed together about the organ issue, for those closely involved like PC Boots, Miss Prickly-Cat, Deirdre Doll — and, especially, about the Referendum.

They had also prayed for the children in the town and for the Vicar and his wife and their family, and for people they knew who were ill or unhappy — including Percy Postman and his dog-phobia, which was making him very miserable. Was the time spent in this way worth it? Was it working? Roddy, for whom this whole exercise was an intriguing new experience, was curious to know whether any results were being achieved. Could they not put an audit in hand to ascertain this?

Bushy-Beard had shuffled uneasily in his chair, embarrassed by his young friend's naïve suggestion. Some others present were shocked and looked away from Roddy. Two or three giggled nervously. But the Vicar smiled at him encouragingly, just as he had at the first meeting when Roddy, feeling carried away by the fervent eloquence of Bushy-Beard's opening prayer, exclaimed at the end, "I'll second that!" while all the others were mumbling correct "Amens". The Vicar stated a little later that Roddy's version was the best modern translation of "Amen" that he'd heard.

Now, again supportively, he said, "Roddy's onto something. There's no point in praying if we don't expect answers."

So they gave time to a thoughtful review, sharing news together. But the "audit" proved somewhat disappointing. The longest report was a remarkably graphic update concerning Percy Postman and his dog problem. Bushy-Beard's account ran as follows:

"I took Percy over to Toyville for a session with the Psychotherapist Dr Fritz Probemeister who happens to be a distant cousin of mine. There's nothing confidential about what followed — Percy is open about the whole thing. Bluntly, it was disastrous from start to finish. First, Fritz said he'd try something called a *desensitization procedure*. Percy was told that he would actually meet a dog at close quarters — under controlled conditions.

"The acute anxiety triggered by this announcement was neutralised — in theory — by some preliminary relaxation techniques. These seemed to work because Percy came over quite drowsy. Then a little floppy-eared spaniel puppy was brought into the consulting-room, and Percy was urged to say Hi and stroke it. The suggestion reduced him to mute terror.

"Fritz calmed him down again, and when the tiny creature advanced tentatively, tail wagging nineteen-to-the-dozen, Percy did, with a supreme effort of will, dangle his hand in front of it. But when the puppy actually licked his finger it was more than he could stand. The scream caused even the Doctor to leap from his chair. The terrified puppy did a convulsive vertical take-off then fled under the table, whimpering with fear and piddling on the carpet.

"For a few minutes the two whimpered *at each other* — the puppy, trembling with apprehension, had rolled onto its back in a suppliant position, paws in the air, eyes pleading. Percy was cowering back on the sofa, legs drawn up, also shaking, and wild-eyed. Fritz is now deeply worried about the possible long-lasting effect on the puppy, which doesn't belong to him, and he's paying for an animal psychologist to treat it.

"In the second session," continued Bushy-Beard, "Fritz changed tack. The approach this time was aimed at replacing Automatic Negative Thoughts (ANTS) with Positive Perceptions which accorded with Reality. Percy was told that he must stop believing the lies he was telling himself about himself — and about all dogs. He needed to re-order his *thoughts* and bring his feelings and attitudes into line with *truth* — about dogs and about 'Life and the Universe and Everything'.

"This seemed to go down quite well, and Percy was nodding in excited agreement. So the good Doctor informed him that during the next appointment he would provide an easy, utterly unthreatening opportunity for him to actually prove, in practice, the effectiveness of this … dognitive behaviour therapy, I think he called it.

"It turned out to be an unwise procedure. On reflection, it was almost certainly premature. Come the following Tuesday, Fritz spent the first half-hour going over old ground — 'as you think, so you are' — 'mind over matter' — 'talk truth to yourself' and so on. Then he opened the door and there entered the room, not a puppy, but a big, soppy golden Labrador called Sophie, padding her way amiably towards Percy, surveying him with friendly soft brown eyes, head bowed obsequiously, tail gently waving. But Percy, sweating with the effort, just could not Tell Himself The Truth that the brute had no intention of suddenly springing upon him and tearing him apart with its fearsome jaws — and ran out through the open door.

"He vowed never to return to Fritz's consulting-room, but he did go back — and events have taken a strange, worrying turn. Encouraged to reflect on the encounter with

Sophie and especially upon the dog's eirenic and reproachful gaze he concluded that the creature had been deliberately mocking him, humiliating him, showing him up. Prompted by Fritz's probing, he came to realise, he says, that underlying his fear of dogs was a deeply-buried anger. It all went back — he was helped to remember — to an occasion when, aged two years old, he had fallen over and was crying with a grazed knee, and the family dog came and stood over him wuffing with gleeful amusement and wagging its tail with malicious happiness.

"This had set the pattern for ensuing years — right up to the week before. The brute in Fritz's room had been actually *laughing at him*, sneering, taking the mickey, *reducing* him... All along, through the years, it had been the dogs' fault, not his. With the Doctor's help, he has been able to own these newly-uncovered emotions of resentful hostility towards dogs in general, and seen through their malign efforts to induce feelings of inferiority and fear in him. Yes, the dogs were to blame — not him. It was a case of canine conning.

"That's where it has all got out of hand. Excited by these new insights, Percy was deaf to Fritz's talk of Anger Management and Coping Strategies and Coming To Terms with the Unconscious Causes of his strong emotions... Seething with released, unbridled rage repressed through the years by an unwarranted self-reproach and self-blame, he's now going to get even with the whole kingdom of canines. Rather than *freeze*, or take *flight*, he's going to *fight* with adrenaline-fuelled fury every dog he meets. Maybe kill it. You can see the problems. There are rocks ahead. Fritz rang me about it, very worried. 'That way madness lies' he says, fearing a wave of vengeful dog-carnage, I suppose."

Bushy-Beard paused.

"No, I'm afraid it seems that our prayerful concern for Percy has so far proved ineffectual. In fact, I blame myself for making matters worse. If I had not taken him to Fritz..."

There were murmurs of dissent around the room. Nobody blamed Bushy-Beard. But a mood of despondency descended upon them, deepened by hearing that there was equally disheartening news concerning Miss Prickly-Cat and Constable Boots who, aided and abetted by the Gremlins, continued to be obstructive — even aggressive. And letters continued to be pushed through the Vicarage letterbox.

The Referendum, when it took place, had resulted in mixed signals. In itself, it was remarkably positive: those voting For an electric blower — 67; those Against — 8.

But unaccountably, the Church Council voted to disregard the figures on the grounds that they were misleading. After the meeting, members themselves were confused as to how this strange decision had been arrived at and how it could possibly be made comprehensible to the church and community at large. They did recall that Shifty and Sarky had been very vocal and persuasive throughout the meeting, so the two Gremlins were asked to produce an explanatory memorandum for wide distribution. ("The Council's spin-doctors," Bushy-Beard had explained to Roddy.) It read as follows:

> The Church Council has given full and concentrated consideration to the results of the Referendum related to the proposal to install an electrically-powered mechanical blower in the church organ. Those results reveal a substantial majority in favour of such a device. Members were deeply moved by this clear expression of loving concern for our esteemed friend and Community Police Officer, Constable Boots, and the compassionate recognition that an electrically powered blower would relieve him of the taxing expenditure of energy Sunday by

Sunday in manually pumping the instrument.

However, Council members were also reminded of PC Boots' praiseworthy desire to continue this service, and his stated reluctance to be the cause of incurring considerable expense to the church. He wished to reassure everyone that he enjoyed robust health. And for him, the preservation of worthy music, undiluted by modern developments, was of first importance.

Clearly, not all who voted will have been, could have been, cognisant of these crucial factors, which cast an altogether different light on their concerns. The Council's decision to overrule the result of the Referendum will therefore be seen as informed, wise and forward-looking.

So nothing had changed. All in all, the whole Tuesday evening thing had not seemed to be such a big deal: this was the unspoken thought of most of those sitting in the glum circle later. Not so, Roddy.

"I don't know how to put this," he volunteered, hesitantly, "but *I* feel different. And I think we've all changed. I've *noticed* that we have — maybe because it's all such a new experience for me, to hear people talking to God *together*. We were friends before, but somehow the friendship is deeper now. And — well, I just want to say — that I reckon these evenings *have* been worth it, we *are* being listened to — and yes, I believe God is *real*. That's amazing! I'm sure things *will* happen. But even if they don't, it's been so worthwhile because we've been, yes, talking to him together, and it's been great and maybe we should just thank him for *that*... He *is* here. I know it..."

In the silence that followed, the whole atmosphere changed. After a short while the Vicar said, "Good on you, Roddy," and, reaching for his guitar in the corner of the room, "let's have a time of *praise* and *thanksgiving*. As you would say, Colonel — let's *sing*, dammit!"

So they did — and a whole hour of songs and spoken prayers had gone quickly by without anybody noticing it was later than usual. They all left the Vicarage and walked home feeling completely different — buoyant belief was displacing disconsolate doubts. Which was — some might say — illogical, because still nothing had changed.

But soon, various utterly unexpected developments occurred. Were they related in any way to that Tuesday evening? Bushy-Beard vouchsafed to Roddy that they probably were. Roddy was bemused.

First, Miss Prickly-Cat suffered a broken leg.

"Golly!" expostulated Roddy to Bushy-Beard, "none of us would have wished that on the poor soul! We asked for *good* things to happen. D'you think maybe the wires got crossed at heaven's switchboard? I know that quote about things moving in a mysterious way — but I'm not sure I follow…"

Bushy-Beard replied gently to his young friend, saying lots of wise things about prayer and providence, and ended by quoting a verse from the bible about *all* things working together for good to those who love God — "and Miss Prickly-Cat does love him, Roddy…"

Bushy-Beard's words were to prove prophetic in a remarkable way. The first development was that loads of people from the church visited Miss Prickly-Cat in Playville General Hospital with flowers and grapes and chocolates, and magazines for her to read. Lots of other people also sent Get-Well cards. Soon, her room was festooned. A nurse told the Vicar — who, with his wife, called and chatted and prayed with her every day — that one evening she had found Miss Prickly-Cat quietly crying and saying, "I can't believe it … can't believe it … *so* kind … such kindness."

The second major happening was Police Constable Boots' promotion — to Detective Sergeant. The townsfolk were delighted for him, and for themselves. What an honour — for him and for Playville! A special Public Meeting was called in the Town Hall. The Chief Constable came and made a speech in praise of PC Boots' sterling service, of which the elevation to a higher rank was a recognition from Headquarters.

The Vicar, on behalf of everyone, congratulated "Detective Sergeant Boots", spoke of the pride felt by the whole community, and presented him with a fine new clock for the Police Station (the old one, known as 'Grantchester' had registered the same time, mid-afternoon, for as long as anyone could remember). After thunderous applause and prolonged affectionate cheers, the Detective Sergeant stood to speak but clearly found it difficult to find words. Feelings of wonder and gratitude had welled up and threatened to undermine his normal rock-like composure. But he did say a few sentences expressing gratitude, and sat down amidst more acclamation.

"Guess what" said Bushy-Beard. Roddy was again sitting in his friend's comfortable lounge sharing coffee and doughnuts. Two weeks had passed.

"Tell me," requested Roddy.

"The Vicar rang just before you arrived. Miss Prickly-Cat *and* Sergeant Boots have withdrawn their objections. The Colonel, bless him, has said that he'll stump up the cash needed for the electric motor. So Mr Moneybags is happy. But in fact, lots of other donations are promised. An Extraordinary Meeting of the Church Council has been called — the project is certain to be approved. Nothing the Gremlins can do about it. The Archdeacon has given his go-ahead — 'what a happy issue out of our afflictions' he says. A Faculty won't be necessary — he's happy to issue a

Certificate of Authorisation. We've even planned a big Thanksgiving-cum-Dedication service for two months from now. And the Bishop will be invited!"

"Sorted!" cried Roddy exultantly, but suddenly went quiet. As did Bushy-Beard. They were remembering Tuesday evenings.

Chapter 5

Roddy Gets the Message

On that Sunday morning two months later, the church was again full, this time for the great service of Thanksgiving and Dedication. The organ, which had also received a thorough overhaul and been re-tuned, as well as receiving a new electrically-powered blowing mechanism, sounded marvellous.

The specially written Form of Service included three much-loved traditional hymns: the first, rousing and celebratory; the second, after sensitively scripted prayers of Confession and Thanksgiving led by the Vicar, was movingly meditative and responsive; the third, at the conclusion of the service — to the tune *Diademata* — could have been heard, it was said afterwards, in Toyville. Two passages from the Bible were read: one by Detective Sergeant Boots, the other by Kylie, the oldest of the Tenpin children.

"We're now going to be led in a time of praise by our newly-formed music group," announced the Vicar.

The group, assembled in the chancel, astonished everyone. It comprised the Vicar himself with his guitar; Mrs Tilly Tenpin, flautist; Ernie Elephant, percussion; five children with recorders; Mr Bottle, violin (!); the Colonel, cello; Mademoiselle Fifi with her accordion; and Bessie Bear on piano. There was an unbelieving, expectant hush. Then Mademoiselle Fifi took over.

"*Eh bien, Bessie*, 'it it. Key of F — 'When ze saints go marching in'. *Un, deux — un, deux, trois.*"

And hit it, Bessie did. Roddy was amazed and entranced, tapping his toes — as was every person in the church. Soon everyone was on their feet. In perfect time and flawless harmony, following the lead given by accordion and piano, the group lifted the whole congregation into a sound of singing which rang and echoed round the building. Other praise-songs followed and then, just before the prayers (composed and read by Bushy-Beard), two quiet, reflective songs were sung, and there was such a peace — and awareness of a Presence — that an unplanned time of profound silence followed.

Then —

"Before the Bishop preaches," said the Vicar, fully aware that his words would cause disbelief and wonder, "we listen to a contribution to our service from our dear friend Miss Prickly-Cat. We are all so glad that she has made a complete recovery from her injury. Now, not everyone will know that Miss Prickly-Cat is a trained singer of considerable fame, notably as the leading contralto with the county's much-travelled Philharmonic Orchestra and Choir.

"She has chosen to sing for us, this morning, the lovely aria from the oratorio 'Elijah' — 'O rest in the Lord, wait patiently for him'. She wishes me to say that this is, for her, an act of heartfelt thanksgiving."

As the gentle organ accompaniment began, you could have heard a pin drop. And at the end, moved by the sheer beauty of Mendelssohn's music and Miss Prickly-Cat's voice, and the singer's transformed demeanour, and the import of the words and the wonder of the significance of the whole service — there was not a dry eye in the church. (As Bushy-Beard remarked to Roddy the following day, "Six months ago we would have heard 'Hailstones and coals of fire'!").

The Bishop declared that not for a very long time had he felt so caught up, "spiritually refreshed and invigorated" by exuberant, God-honouring praise; nor so inspired by worship which also reflected "the beauty of holiness". He encouraged them to put the past behind and move forward into the future with faith and joy and, above all, in love — among themselves and for the whole community of Playville.

This love should be shown by continuing compassionate service to all fellow citizens, and relevant evangelism supported by people-friendly church services which met the needs of all ages and stages, from small children to senior citizens … fresh expressions of the old, old story.

"Today it has been my pleasure to re-dedicate this organ. As its potential, its musicality, has been released and beautified by new power within it, so may you all be lifted into new life, new love, new exploits, by the divine power in you and among you."

The last hymn was accompanied by every musical instrument in the building, and everyone sang their heart out. "A bit like Psalm 150," whispered Bushy-Beard.

Roddy looked it up later, and agreed.

Roddy had many chats with his friend in the days and weeks following that memorable service. People of all ages were attending church Sunday by Sunday, in growing numbers — they used only one book now (plus Bibles in the pews).

A screen and modern projector helped with the songs and the singing. Organ and music group continued in happy cooperation. And the weekly Tuesday meeting for praise and prayer now filled the large Vicarage lounge.

Sadly, Shifty and Sarky the Gremlins, only turned up sporadically in church and though warmly welcomed, always left muttering to each other. And Mr Mopey continued to utter fairly regular gloomy prognostications like, "It won't last" and "The bubble will burst" and — about the organ and its new motor — "I just hope we're fully insured."

Roddy himself could hardly believe the changes in his life — "in myself and in how I spend my time, and so many real friends and new things to enjoy. *Everything's* different," as he put it to Bushy-Beard. "Best of all, I've met that Person you told me about. I know who he is. I've got so much to learn — but the Vicar's Christian Foundations Course is a wow! Wonders will never cease."

"Which reminds me," said Bushy-Beard, "there's been another wonder. Have you heard about Percy Postman? No? Roddy, it's amazing. I'll keep it brief. Last week Bonzo, the Vicarage dog, fell ill — went all weak and floppy — couldn't stand up on its legs. The vet had to be called in. As you can imagine, the Vicar's children were desolate. One morning, Percy called with the post a few minutes before they left for school and — you know what kids are like — they told him all about Bonzo.

"Blissfully ignorant of the Percy-dog-saga, they say, 'Percy, *do* come in and see him and try and cheer him up and help him to be better. He'll like *you*.' Well, taking his hand — so how could he refuse — they lead him to where the dog is lying in his big basket. The kids kneel down and say, 'Bonzo, here's Percy come to see you.' Bonzo just about lifts his big black head, gives a kind of dog-smile, wags his tail feebly once and drops off to sleep again.

"And do you know what happened next, Roddy? The Vicar who was quietly standing in the doorway told me — Percy crouched down with the children and said quietly, 'Oh, poor old Bonzo … get better soon,' *and then he reached out his hand and stroked the dog's head.* After a day or two Bonzo recovered, and they're the best of friends!"

Roddy was flabbergasted. "That caps the lot! Now I can

believe nothing is impossible. *Anyone* can change — *be* changed."

Bushy-Beard smiled.

"You've got the message, Roddy."

More books from White Tree Publishing

Bible People Real People
J Stafford Wright   ISBN 9-780-9525-9565-6
(314 pages) An unforgettable who is who in the Bible, Old Testament and New.

Christians and the Supernatural
J Stafford Wright   ISBN 9-780-9525-9564-9
(224 pages) A key to understanding mysterious events.

English Hexapla — the Gospel of John
Chris Wright   ISBN 978-0-9525956-1-8 (152 large pages)
The full text of Bagster's assembled work for the Gospel of John, with the words of the six most important translations of the New Testament into English, made between 1380 and 1611. Below the English is the original Greek text after Scholz.

Help!
Chris Wright   ISBN 978-0-9927642-2-7 (42 pages)
*Can I be sure I'm a Christian and going to heaven? *I'm definitely a Christian, but now I seem to be stuck. Why? *I used to believe, but what's happened to the faith I once had? Do you sometimes ask yourself one of these questions? If you do, you're not alone.

Locked Door Shuttered Windows
J Stafford Wright   ISBN: 9-781-4791-1543-3 (206 pages)
Christian Fiction. What is inside the fascinating house with the locked door and the shuttered windows? Satan wants an experiment. God allows it.

So, What Is a Christian?
Chris Wright   ISBN 978-0-9927642-3-4 (38 pages)
Explains what defines a Christian, and how to take the first step to new life.

Starting Out
Chris Wright   ISBN 978-0-9927642-1-0 (38 pages)
For young people starting the Christian life, although new Christians of any age should find it helpful. Or maybe you started the Christian life some time ago, but feel you have never really moved forward. Then this book is also for you.

The Simplicity of the Incarnation
J Stafford Wright   ISBN 9-780-9525-9563-2
(166 pages) "I believe in ... Jesus Christ ... born of the Virgin Mary." A beautiful stained glass image, or a medical reality? This is the choice facing Christians today. Can we truly believe that two thousand years ago a young woman, a virgin named Mary, gave birth to the Son of God? The answer is simple: we can.

White Tree Publishing for younger readers

Agathos, The Rocky Island, and Other Stories
Chris Wright   ISBN 978-0-9525956-8-7 (146 pages)
Once upon a time there were two favourite books for Sunday reading: Parables From Nature and Agathos and The Rocky Island. These books contained all sorts of short stories, usually with a hidden meaning. In this illustrated book there is a selection of the very best of these stories, carefully retold to preserve the feel of the originals, coupled with ease of reading and understanding for today's readers and listeners.

Mary Jones and Her Bible — An Adventure Book
Chris Wright   ISBN 978-0-9525956-2-5 (158 pages)
The reader will really feel they are taking part with the true story of Mary Jones as she struggles to buy a Bible of her own. With plenty of photographs of the places that Mary knew so well, and an assortment of puzzles, this book will be remembered for a long time.

Pilgrim's Progress — An Adventure Book
Chris Wright   ISBN 978-0-9525956-6-3 (174 pages)
Travel with young Christian as he sets out on a difficult and perilous journey to find the King. Solve the puzzles and riddles along the way, and help Christian reach the Celestial City. Then travel with his friend Christiana. She has four young brothers who can sometimes be a bit of a problem.

Pilgrim's Progress — Special Edition
Chris Wright   ISBN 978-0-9525956-7-0 (276 pages)

Told in the first person, this book for all ages is a great choice for young readers, as well as for families, Sunday school teachers, and anyone who wants to read John Bunyan's Pilgrim's Progress in a clear form. All the old favourites are here: Christian, Christiana, the Wicket Gate, Interpreter, Hill Difficulty with the lions, the four sisters at the House Beautiful, Vanity Fair, Giant Despair, Faithful and Talkative – and, of course, Greatheart.

Zephan and the Vision
Chris Wright   ISBN 978-0-952-5956-9-4 (216 pages)
An exciting story about the adventures of two angels who seem to know

almost nothing – until they have a vision! Two ordinary angels are caring for the distant Planet Eltor, when they get a big shock – they have to take a trip to Planet Earth!

Full details of all these paperback books are on the websites of major internet book sellers, where copies can be purchased. Some titles are available in local bookshops.

www.ingramcontent.com/pod-product-compliance
Lightning Source LLC
Chambersburg PA
CBHW071223130626
46555CB00004B/1824